Stinky Says "It's No Fun Having the Stinkies"

Words by: Marnie Beck

Pictures by: Larisa Kovtun

ISBN 978-1-63844-291-2 (paperback)
ISBN 978-1-63903-426-0 (hardcover)
ISBN 978-1-63844-292-9 (digital)

Christian Faith Publishing, Inc.
832 Park Avenue
Meadville, PA 16335
www.christianfaithpublishing.com

Printed in the United States of America

This book belongs to

"Love one another." John 13:34

To Mikaila, my luminous "Stinky,"
and to Ryan, my winsome "Stinkpot,"
my treasures of love.

—Nana

Written in 2003, author Marnie Beck filed the manuscript. In 2018, she shared it with a friend whose artistic teenage daughter, Larisa Kovtun (astoundingly born in 2003), tackled the project. Larisa surprised Marnie on her seventy-seventh birthday (2020) with amazing drawings depicting all she had written. The story resurrected, a brilliant illustrator launched, Marnie penned more from her reservoir of life's lessons, bringing the message to its fullness.

Her hope is that children will know God is their Heavenly Father. He loves them and knows their names. They can pray anywhere, anytime. He listens!

Acknowledgments

God's gift, my beloved daughter, Michelle, for the blessing of "Stinky" and "Stinkpot," and all her input.

My exceptional granddaughter, Mikaila (Stinky), for her essence, insightful contribution and edits.

My husband, Ralph, for his unwavering, enduring love!

My illustrator's mother, my friend Aleksandra, for her photography expertise (my bio), her godly influence and guidance to Larisa and coaching her to the finish line.

Larisa, my faith has deepened as I watched God's gifts unfold through her endeavors and her character!

My longtime friend, Carol, for her insight, nudges, and prayers—my cheerleader.

Prophetic encouragers: Masterpeace Counselor Stacey, Blessing Man Forrest; Pastors Lee and Rosemary; Stevie Tenderheart, author/publisher for helping a literary novice find her wings.

Lastly, all praise, thanks, and glory to Jesus, my Redeemer and best friend. He fulfills dreams!

It's no fun having the stinkies! That's how KailaCole felt
the day she woke up with a very sore tummy. It hurt
sooooooo bad! The pains were very sharp, and she didn't
feel good at all!

She was tired of the constant trips to the bathroom! A couple of times, she almost didn't make it! She had the stinkies!

Whenever her mom gave her medicine, KailaCole cried, "Do I have to take it, Mommy? It tastes yucky!"

Mom replied, "Yes, KailaCole, you do, if you want to get better. And be sure to never take medicine from anyone except your parents or people we trust."

Warm baths made her feel much better.
After a while, the medicine did help... Mom
was right!

Some kids at school heard KailaCole had the stinkies! Whenever they saw her, they snickered and laughed, often whispering to each other behind her back. Some would even say, "Phew! Did you take a bath this week?"

From then on, they teased her and called her "Stinky!" Shaylyn, the tattletale, teased her the most!

KailaCole, very sad and afraid, waited a long time
before telling anyone!

One day, her mother, noticing her sadness, asked, "KailaCole, is everything okay?"

With a flood of tears, she poured out the whole story!

Her mom said, "I bet you feel better now! I'm proud of you for being so brave. Remember, I'm always here to listen and to care."

The next day, they met with her teacher. KailaCole was a bit nervous but told the whole story, naming all the mean kids.

The teacher met with each one and told them, "What you have been doing to KailaCole is called bullying. It's hurtful and makes people sad. We need to practice the Golden Rule. Treat others like you want to be treated." She warned them, "Bullying is NOT allowed here in school."

Treat others like you want to be treated.

Storytime with Mom was always enjoyable! A few days later, her mother chose a new book about God called *Love Makes Everything Better!* KailaCole was about to learn some wonderful things! Mom read, "God made and loves everything and everyone! God is LOVE! LOVE is GOOD! GOD shares His heart full of LOVE with anyone who prays and asks!" Mom read on, "Praying means talking to God, our Heavenly Father."

KailaCole, excited, said, "Mommy, may we pray?"

"Dear Heavenly Father, would you please give me a love heart like yours, and help me to be nice— EVEN to the mean kids—and, oh yeah, I hope I'm not sad if I'm called 'Stinky'!"

This special book became KailaCole's favorite!

The school bullies were often sneaky and still mean, but KailaCole was NOT mean to them. Instead of tattling, she'd walk away and whisper a prayer, "God, please help the hurt, mean kids to want love hearts."

A bully noticed one day that KailaCole had a bag of candy. He yelled, "Hey, Stinky, how about giving us some?"

Having love in her heart, KailaCole found it easy to share. The mean kids couldn't understand how she could be nice to them when they were so mean to her! Before long, they stopped teasing her.

Because Stinky was a very nice girl, she had many friends! She shared all her toys, and some of the mean kids even became her friends.

Soon, most everyone started calling her "Stinky"—even her mom, Dad, and younger brother, RyRy.

Ry Ry was learning to be nice and to share his toys.

They nicknamed him "Stinkpot" because one day he had the stinkies!

KailaCole began to like her nickname because she liked herself. She was especially glad she seldom had stinky ways anymore.

Even when she played dress-up, she called herself "Princess Stinky" and "Stinky Ballerina."

One day, Stinky planned a special tea party and
decided to invite Shaylyn. The girls waited and waited,
but when she didn't arrive, they began without her.

Just then, Shaylyn's mother phoned. She said, "Shaylyn will not be able to attend the tea party as she has the stinkies!"

Stinky shared the bad news! The girls agreed when she suggested they pray for Shaylyn. Stinkpot, listening, was invited!

Excited, he said, "I'm in, I love to pray but no need to invite ME to the tea party... Yuck, that's girl stuff!"

The girls giggled!

So the tea party became their first ever prayer meeting!

Each one prayed, Stinky adding, "Thank you, dear God, for loving us. And would you please heal Shaylyn without her having to take yucky medicine. And help us all to be nice to one another!"

The next day, Shaylyn, with her mom's okay, raced to Stinky's house! Panting, she squeaked, "Stinky, I'm all better!" She drew a big breath. "AND IT'S NO FUN HAVING THE STINKIES! Sorry I tattled and we made fun of you. Are you mad at me? Please forgive me."

Stinky was SHOCKED! "No, silly!" she exclaimed! "I'm not mad...
ANYMORE! I asked God for a love heart, then it was really easy. I
felt so happy after I forgave you. I'm glad He healed your stinkies."

"Whew!" Shaylyn burst out, "Thank you, Stinky. You're the nicest friend EVER! How can I get a love heart?"

She replied, "Just tell God you're sorry for your stinky ways"— they giggled—"and ask Him to make your heart new and fill it with His love."

After the prayer, LOVE filled the air.

"We need to celebrate!" Stinky announced. "Let's invite friends and play dress-up!"

Jumping for joy, Shaylyn shouted, "Yay, Princess Stinky! And YOU can call me Princess Meanie."

Laughing and hugging, they could hardly wait for the fun to begin.

The good news spread! "Stinky" and "Meanie" became best friends! Others wanted to know how come they were no longer sad but glad. Before long, many kids, even some of the bullies, asked for love hearts!

It was AMAZING!

They all became very good friends, had fun playing together, and were very nice to one another!

Best of all, they had learned...

LOVE MAKES EVERYTHING BETTER!

The End

Visit Us,
Fans of Stinky!

Stinky Has Pillows!

Love Makes
Everything
Better!

About the Author

Author Marion McCallum-Beck, a.k.a. Marnie Beck from Nova Scotia, fulfilled her childhood vow to leave her small town and experience other places. She resides in the beautiful Pacific Northwest with her husband, Ralph Beck (US Coast Guard RTD). She notes finding faith in God to be her most valuable treasure.

CPSIA information can be obtained
at www.ICGtesting.com
Printed in the USA
BVHW050942221121
622229BV00015B/494